TEEN TITANS GO!™

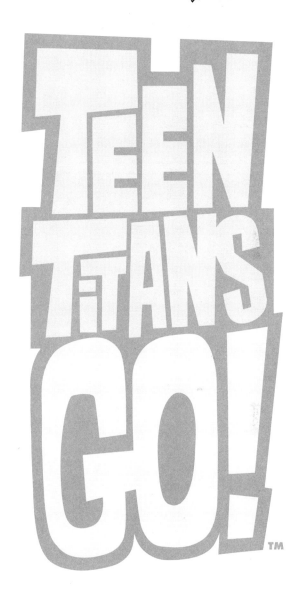

Little, Brown and Company

Hachette Book Group
1290 Avenue of the Americas, New York, NY 10104
Visit us at lb-kids.com

LB kids is an imprint of Little, Brown and Company.
The LB kids name and logo are trademarks of Hachette Book Group, Inc.

The publisher is not responsible for websites (or their content) that are not
owned by the publisher.

First Edition: April 2016

ISBN 978-0-316-33339-9

Library of Congress Control Number: 2014952766

10 9 8 7 6 5 4 3 2 1

CW

Printed in the United States of America

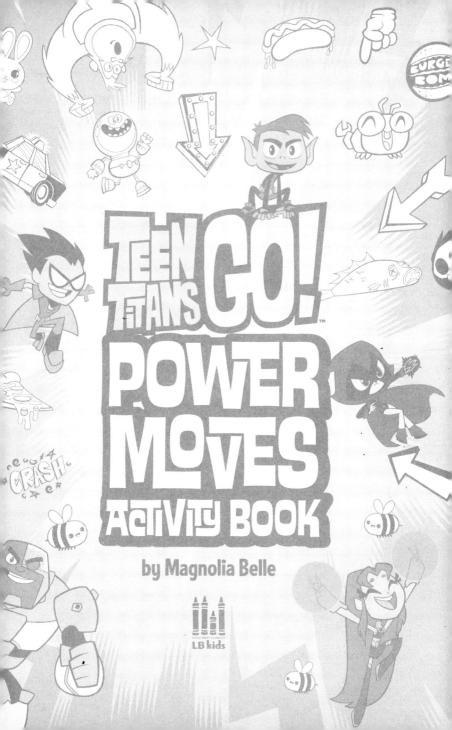

TEEN TITANS GO!™
POWER MOVES
ACTIVITY BOOK

by Magnolia Belle

LB kids

Meet the Teen Titans—the teenage heroes
who protect Jump City from trouble!

Robin is the headstrong leader of the Teen Titans. He has a big
crush on Starfire. She's a wide-eyed princess from outer space!

Raven is Starfire's moody best friend who
can levitate and do magic.

Cyborg is part robot, and
his best bro,
Beast Boy, can shape-shift
into any animal!

When the Titans aren't fighting crime, they like to chill out
at home, where they read books and play video games.
Draw the things you like to do in your free time.

Finish this drawing of Beast Boy!

Who is your favorite Teen Titan?
Draw him or her!

9

Robin needs help decorating his room. Give him a hand by drawing in the posters on his walls.

Beast Boy is practicing his ability to transform into different animals.

Draw some animals you want to see him try!

Something funny is going on in Starfire's room.
Spot the differences and solve who's
behind the mystery!

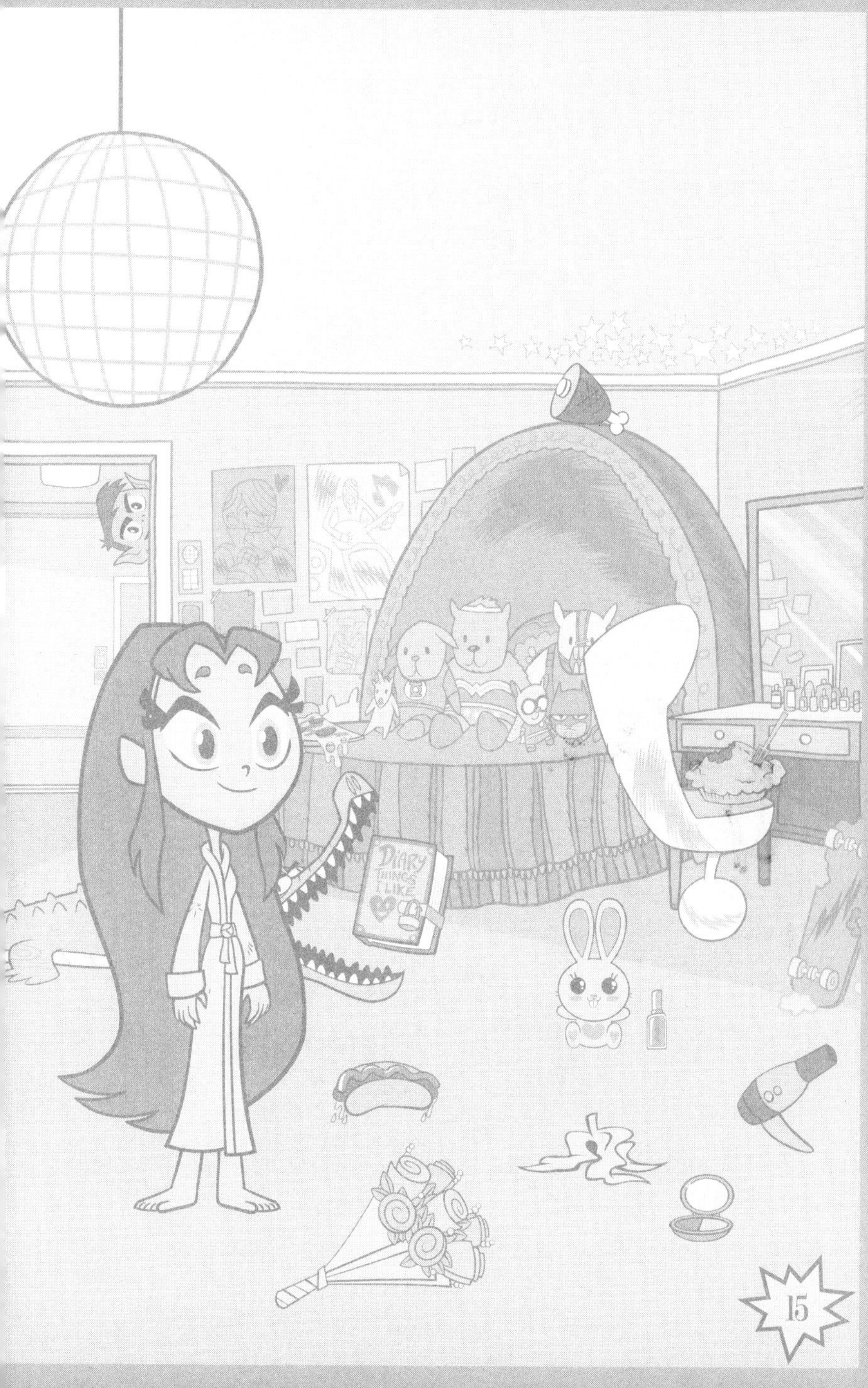
DIARY
THINGS I LIKE

**The Titans are holding tryouts for new members.
Draw yourself as a super hero to see if you make the cut!
Write your super hero name, too!**

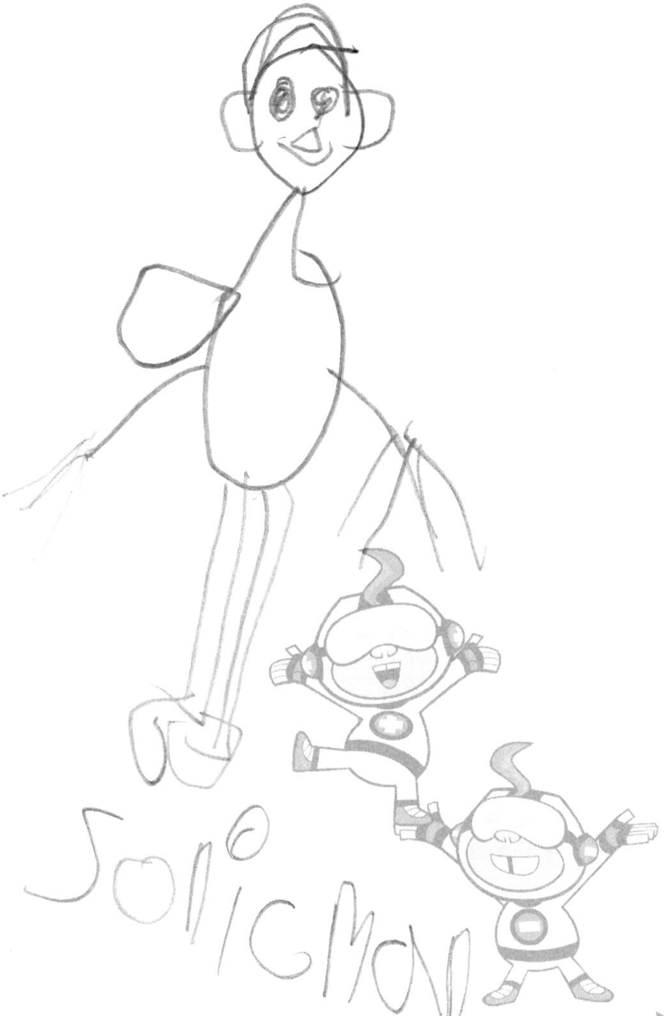

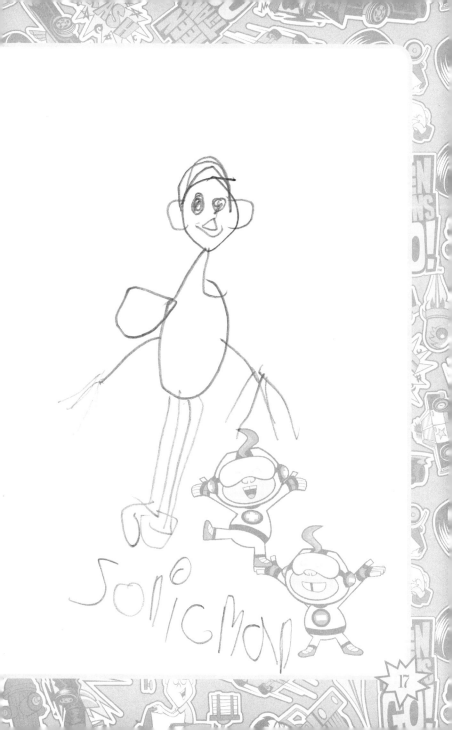

Oh no! Starfire's pet, Silkie, is lost in Titans Tower! Help the Titans find him!

START

START

START

START

START

FINISH!

Draw Raven, Beast Boy, and Cyborg in the kitchen putting together a legendary sandwich.

Draw the ingredients for the greatest sandwich ever.

Strawberry Jelly

Pasta Sauce

The Titans got their uniforms all mixed up!
Draw each Titan with a different hero's uniform!

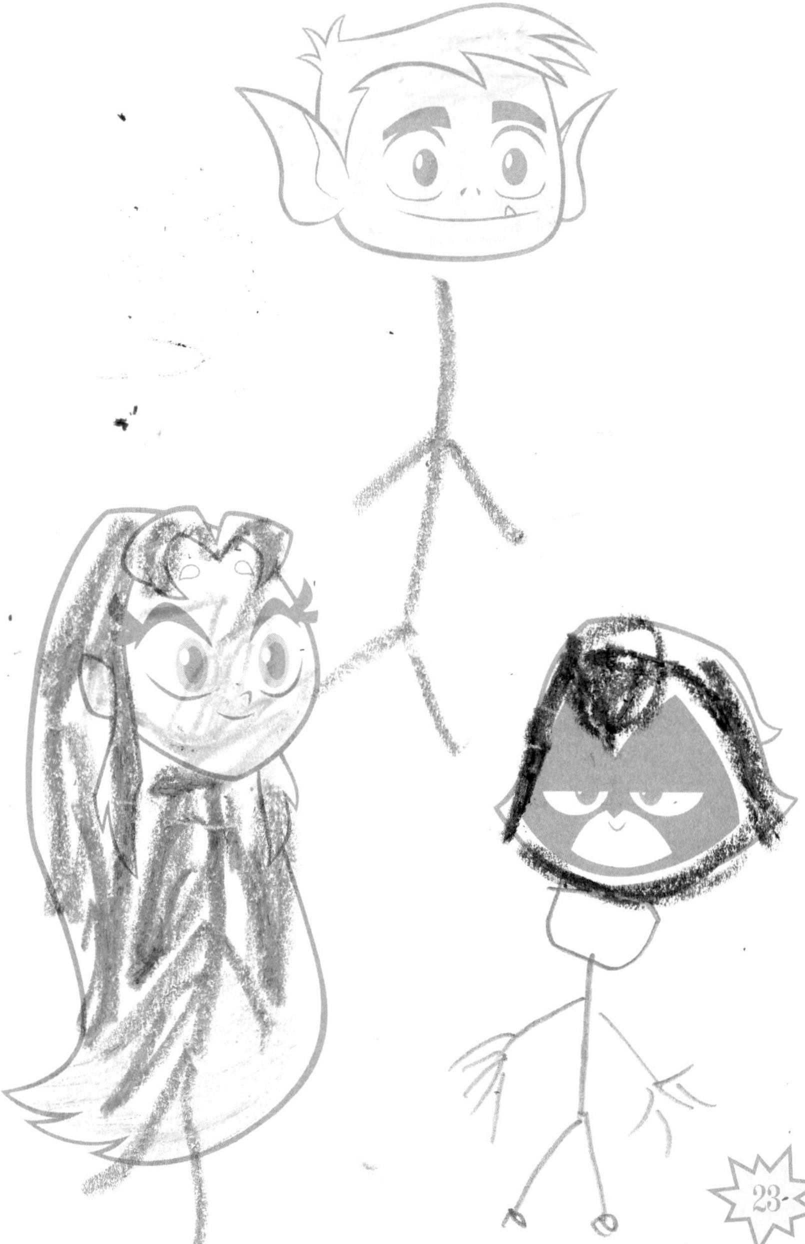

Finish this drawing of Robin!

Robin's feeling bummed that he's the only Titan without superpowers, so Raven uses her magic to give him some. Draw Robin with the powers you would give him!

A red alert goes off within the Tower!
Somebody's robbing a bank downtown.
The Titans need to get there fast, but
Cyborg's car needs repairs.

Draw the Teen Titans a super-speedy new vehicle!

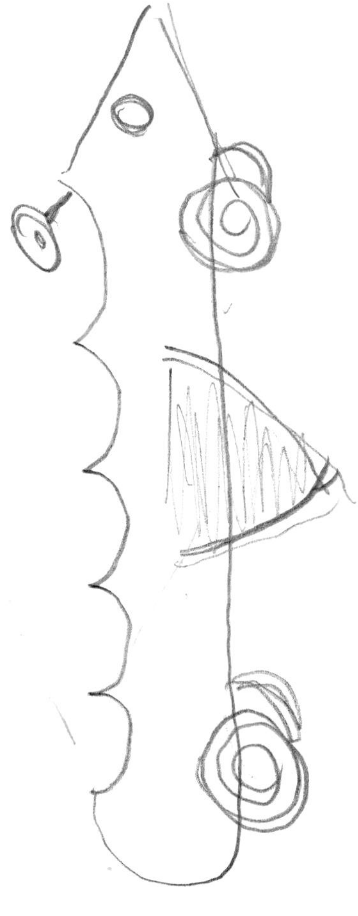

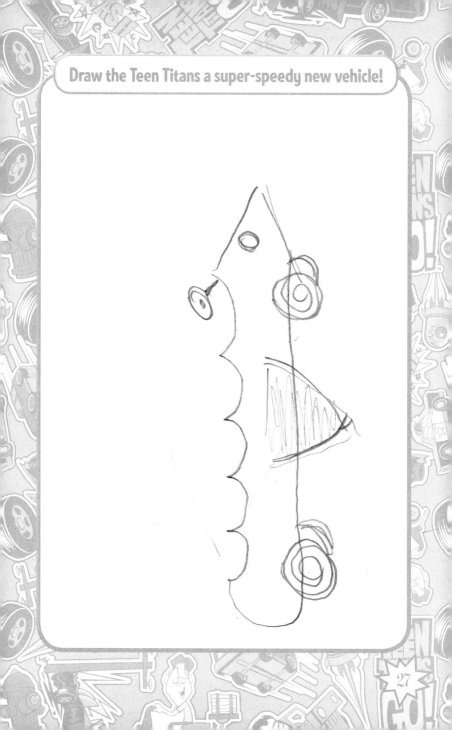

The villainous magician Mumbo,
aka "the Amazing Mumbo Jumbo,"
is using his magic to rob Jump City Bank!

Draw a vault and bags of money floating through the air into Mumbo's hat.

Robin decides to take a more peaceful approach to fighting crime and tries to make Mumbo laugh by telling him jokes.

What do you call a cow with no legs?

GROUND BEEF!
THAT'S RICH!

Say, Mumbo, does your face hurt?

'CAUSE IT'S KILLING ME!

What are some jokes that might make Mumbo laugh?

Mumbo casts a spell and turns the bank into a carnival to slow down the Titans!

Fill the bank with rad carnival rides and attractions.
Turn the bank patrons into clowns and carnies!

Oh no! The Teen Titans are lost in a funhouse! Draw each Titan's silly reflection in the funhouse mirrors!

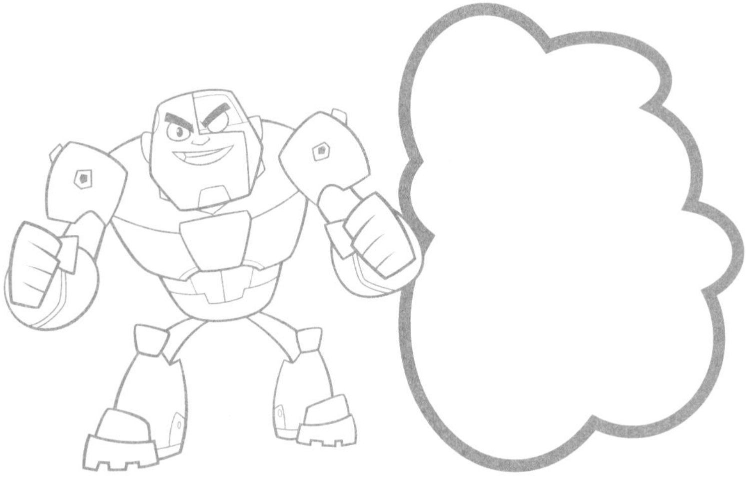

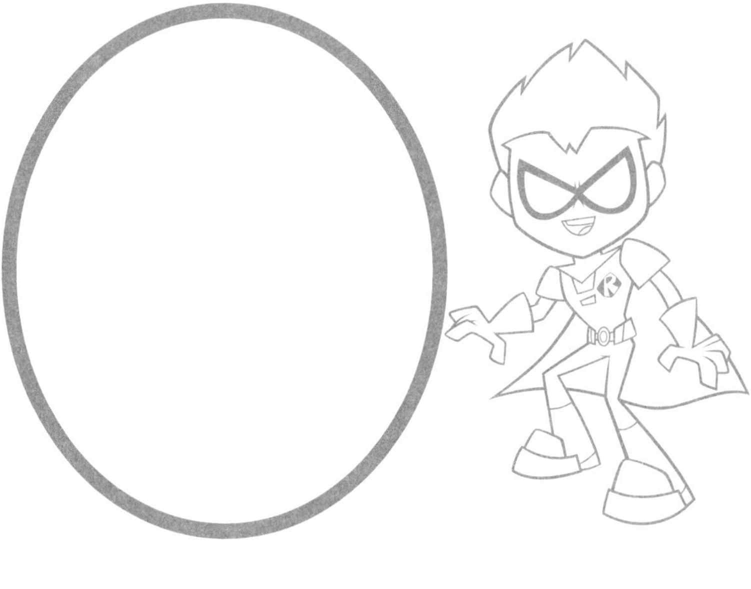

Robin and Starfire are on the Tunnel o' Love ride.
A big, creepy monster pops up and scares them!

What do you think the monster looks like?

Cyborg and Beast Boy stop at a food
stand to get burgers and burritos.

Draw the ingredients to make the best burgers and burritos!

39

Raven is stuck in a ball pit, but there's something else in there with her! What is it? Is it scary? Is it funny? You decide!

The Teen Titans find a bag of money on the sidewalk and return it to the bank, but along the way they daydream about what they would buy with that much money.

What would you buy?

Finish this drawing of Starfire!

Raven is casting spells! Write the magic words Raven uses for her spell, and draw something peculiar appearing out of her spell book.

The Titans need to catch up with Mumbo, so they borrow some sweet go-karts.

Draw a very special go-kart for each Titan!

A NEWS REPORTER FROM THE *JUMP CITY JOURNAL* SNAPS PHOTOS OF THE TEEN TITANS FIGHTING CRIME.

DRAW THE TITANS EXECUTING SOME RAD FIGHTING MOVES FOR THE NEWSPAPER!

Oh no! Mumbo is breaking all the super-villains out of Jump City Jail!

Draw the villains making a run for it.

Cyborg and Beast Boy construct giant burger and burrito monsters to battle each other to prove which is the best food ever.

Design your own food monster for this contest!

Cinderblock escaped from jail, and he's trashing the Jump City power plant.

Finish drawing Robin's motorcycle so he can take care of Cinderblock!

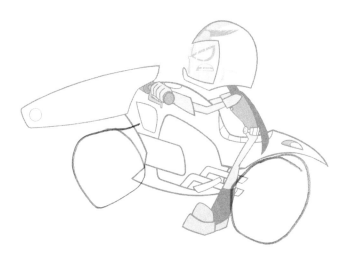

Cyborg invents an app called the Love Matcher 5000 to show the Teen Titans their true super hero soul mates.

Who (or what) do you think would be the perfect match for each Titan? Draw other perfect matches!

Raven and Aqualad get into a scuffle with some rowdy pirates!

Draw a band of scurvy scalawags for Raven and Aqualad to tangle with.

The Teen Titans chase Control Freak into an arcade, where he zaps them into a video game!

Draw the 8-bit Titans
battling pixelated villains.

The Teen Titans drop by Batman's Batcave to borrow some gear to aid in the recapture of the rest of the escaped villains.

Draw the gadgets and weapons they find.

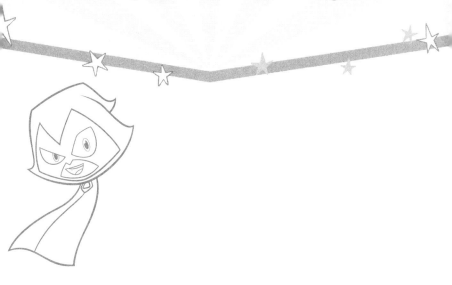

63

The Teen Titans are all discombobulated!
Find them and other stuff in this word search!

STARFIRE

POWER MOVES

RAVEN

BURRITO

ROBIN

BURGER

CYBORG

AQUALAD

BEAST BOY

JINX

SILKIE

TRIGON

```
P E R E G R U B E Y
O R L G T B X I R D
W I Y B T R K N Y B
E F D R U L I O I G
R R D A I R B G R J
M A N S L T R O O R
O T R E S A B I O N
V S M A V Y U B T K
E N E L C A I Q G O
S B Y M R N R L A R
```

65

Beast Boy is having a nightmare where all the Teen Titans turn into zombies. Draw the zombie Titans!

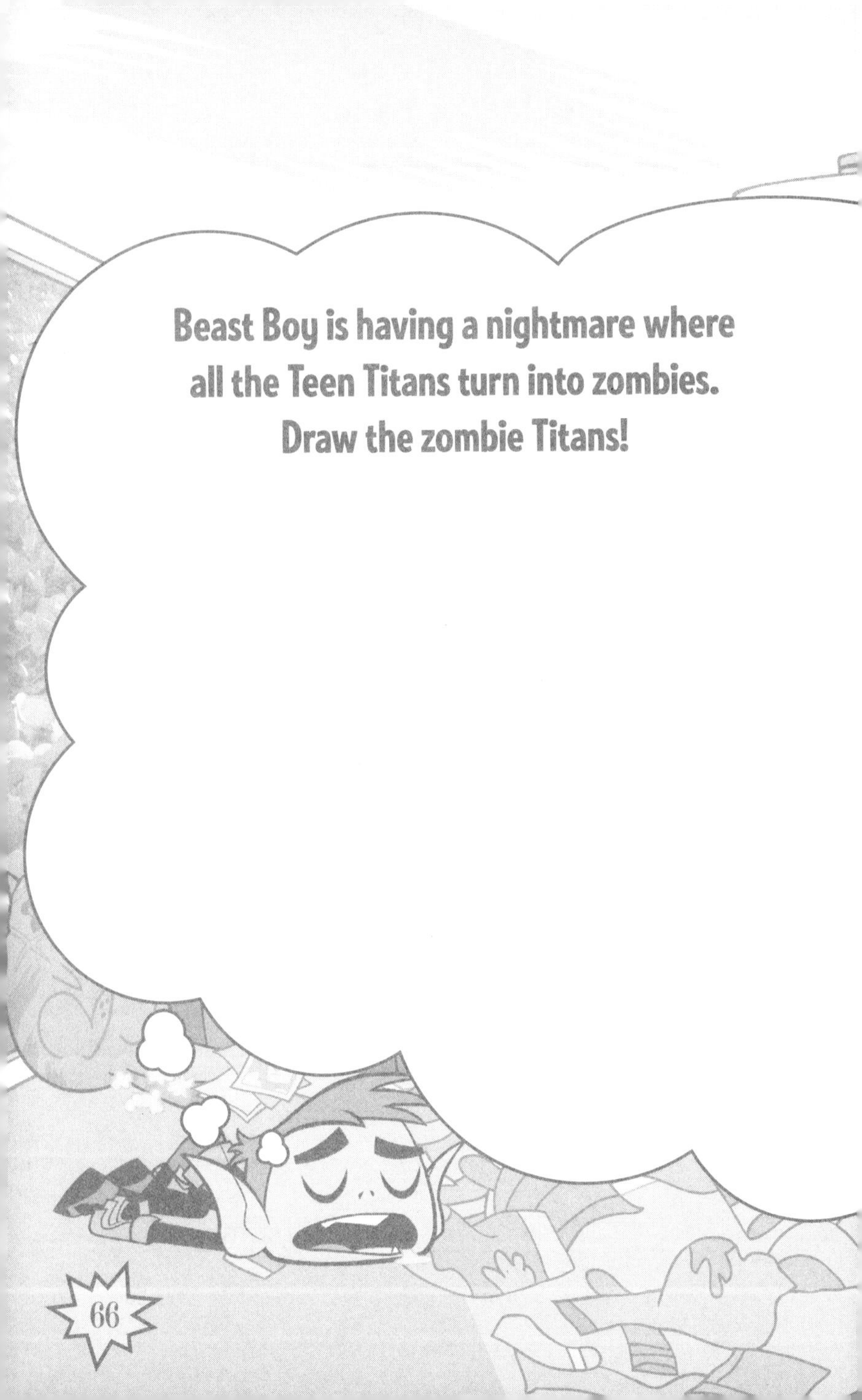

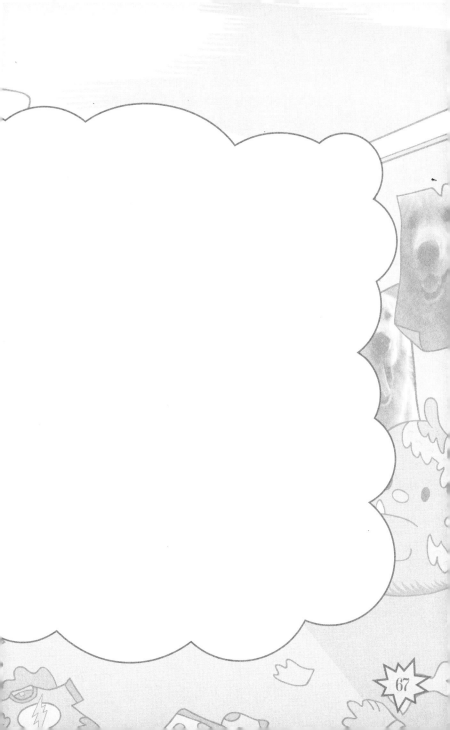

Mother Mae-Eye captures the Teen Titans, and she's baking them into pies! Finish drawing the Titan pies and the rest of the Titan pie factory!

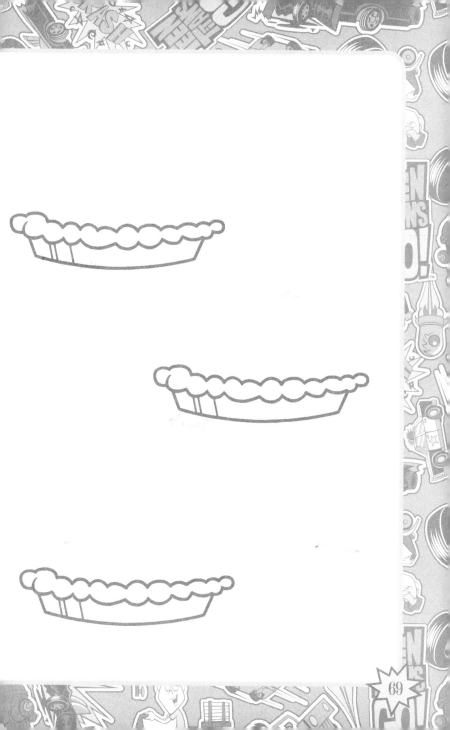

The gang catches up with Mumbo, but he uses his magic to give them all mustaches!

Draw mustaches or beards on all the Teen Titans.

One of Raven's spells backfires and combines all her friends into one hero. Draw the Franken-Titan!

71

Starfire is throwing a big party and inviting all the coolest super heroes. Draw the party attendees.

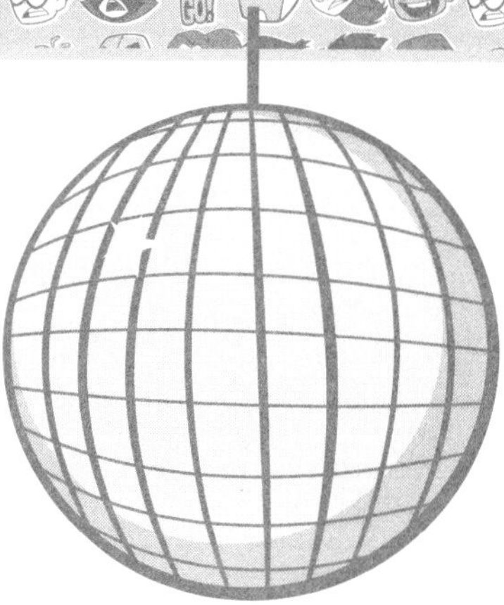

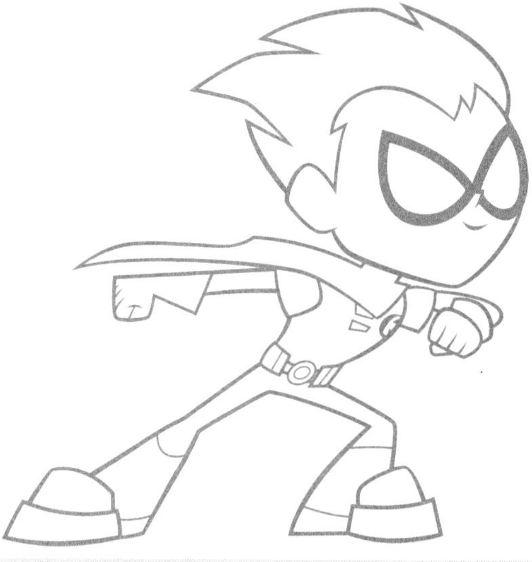

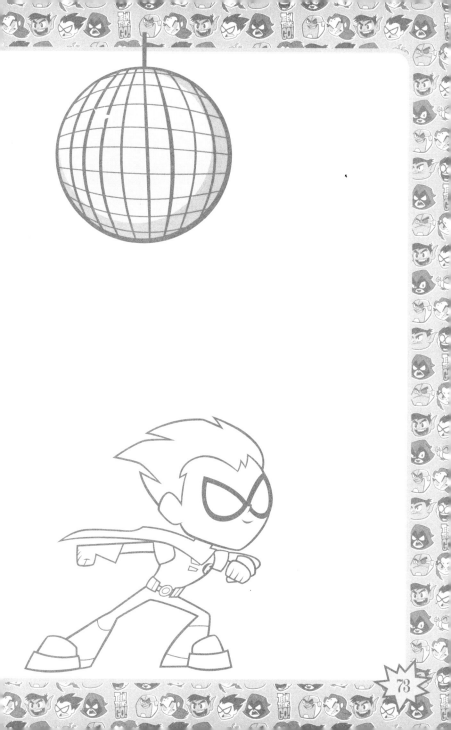

The Teen Titans need to disguise themselves as villains to infiltrate the H.I.V.E. Five headquarters. Make the Titans look more villainous!

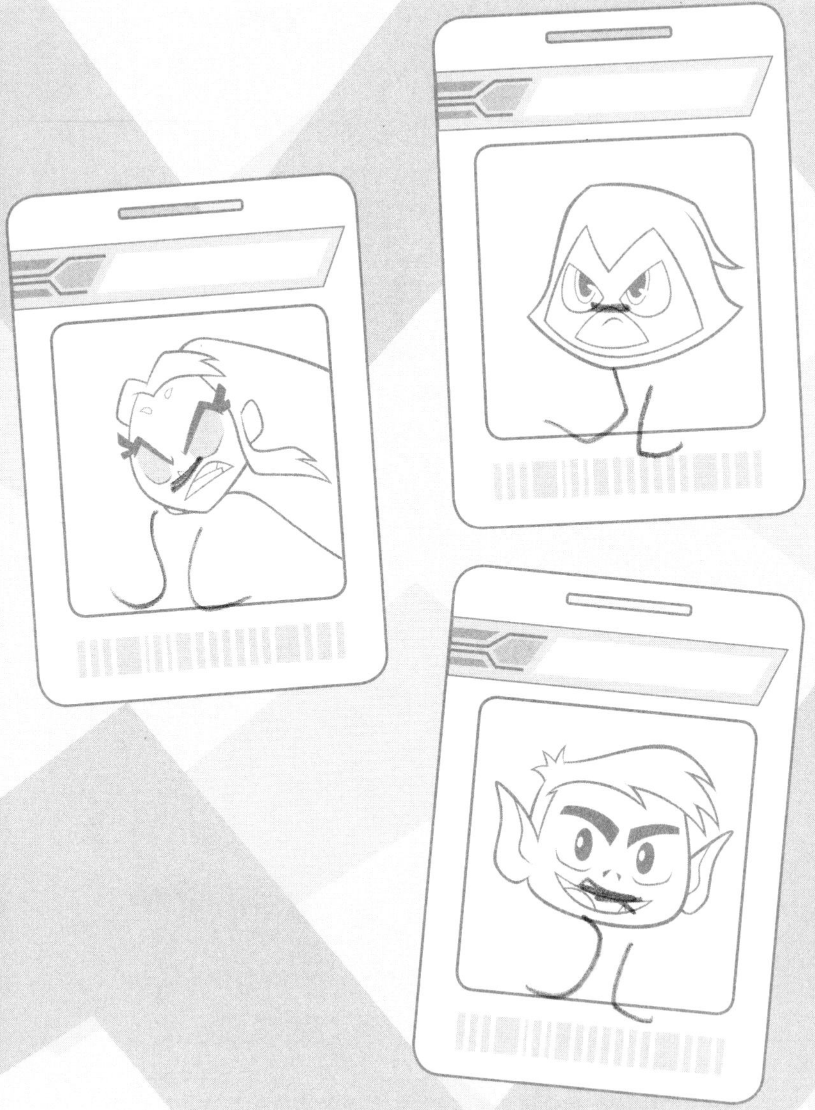

Beast Boy is going doggone crazy digging up
holes all over the yard outside Titans Tower.
Draw the treasures he's found buried in the yard.

Finish this drawing of Raven!

**Robin's favorite bo staff breaks
in the middle of a battle!
Draw some new weapons he can use.**

The Puppet King turns the Teen Titans into puppets!

Finish drawing the puppet versions of the Titans!

Cyborg and Beast Boy abuse Raven's magic to clone themselves.

See how many Cyborgs and Beast Boys you can draw here.

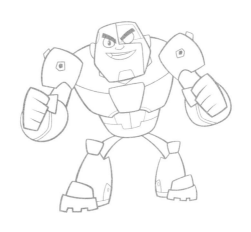

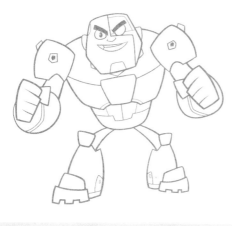

Starfire is cooking a big feast for her friends, but they're in for a surprise–it's all Tamaranian food!

Circle the foods that only a Tamaranian (or Silkie) would love.

It's Halloween, and the Teen Titans
are going trick-or-treating!

Draw the Titans in their costumes!

Mumbo uses his magic to make Titans Tower disappear!
Use the magic of your drawing skills to put it back!

Silkie wants to try some new looks!
Draw some different hair and accessories to see
what really fits his personality.

The Titans are having a pet show to decide
who has the coolest buddy.

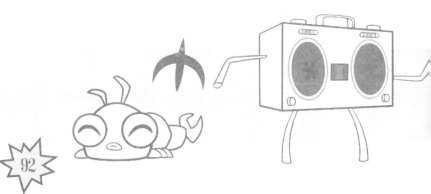

**Draw your buddy and see how well it does!
If you don't have a pet, make one up!**

93

The Teen Titans find themselves in the clutches of the fashionably hip villain Mad Mod, and he's forcing them to play in a band!

Draw the Titans with instruments so they can bop out some swingin' beats!

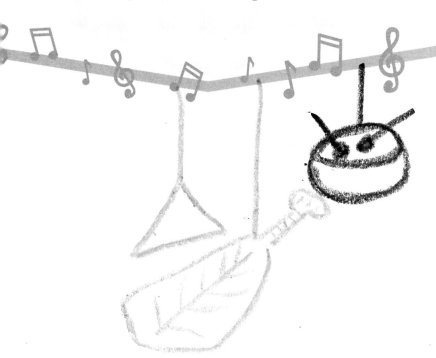

All the Teen Titans are spending the afternoon reading. They love books!

Draw in the covers of the books you think they would read. Don't forget to add the titles!

Blackfire comes to visit her sister, Starfire, and she has gifts for everyone—big, ugly sweaters!

Draw the Titans in their new sweaters.

Robin is taking driving lessons! Unfortunately, he's not a very good driver yet. Draw all the damage he causes to the driving course.

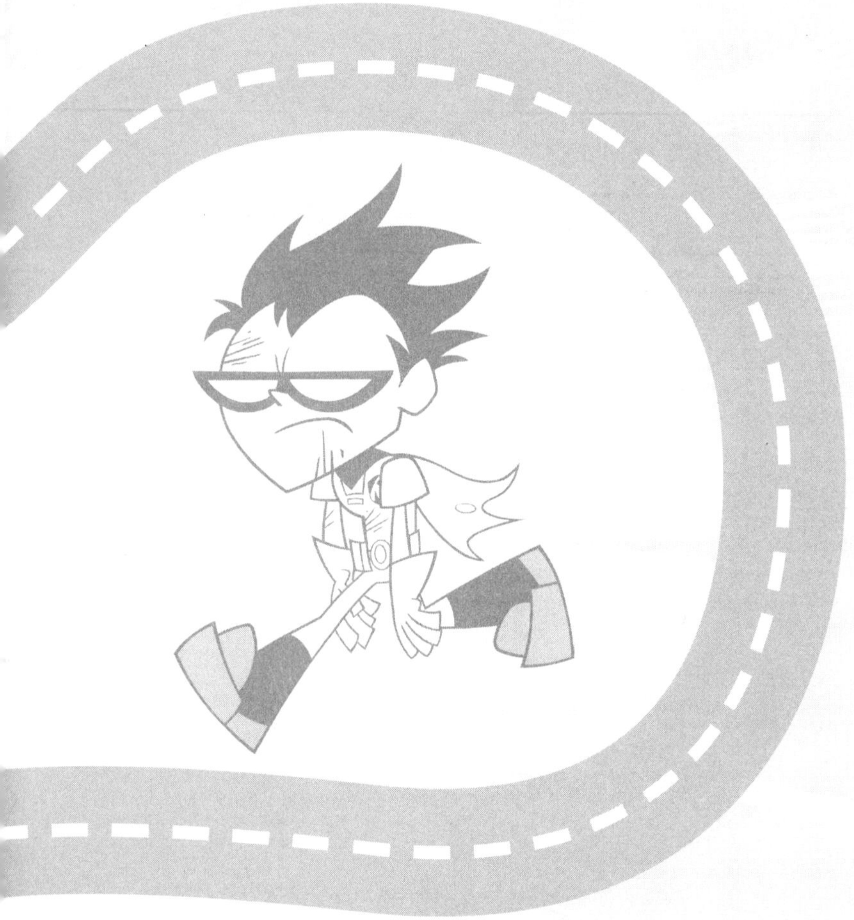

Beast Boy and Cyborg accidentally travel ahead in time and bump into their future selves.

What do the Teen Titans of the future look like?

Now's your chance to jump into the storyteller's seat and make a real Teen Titans comic!

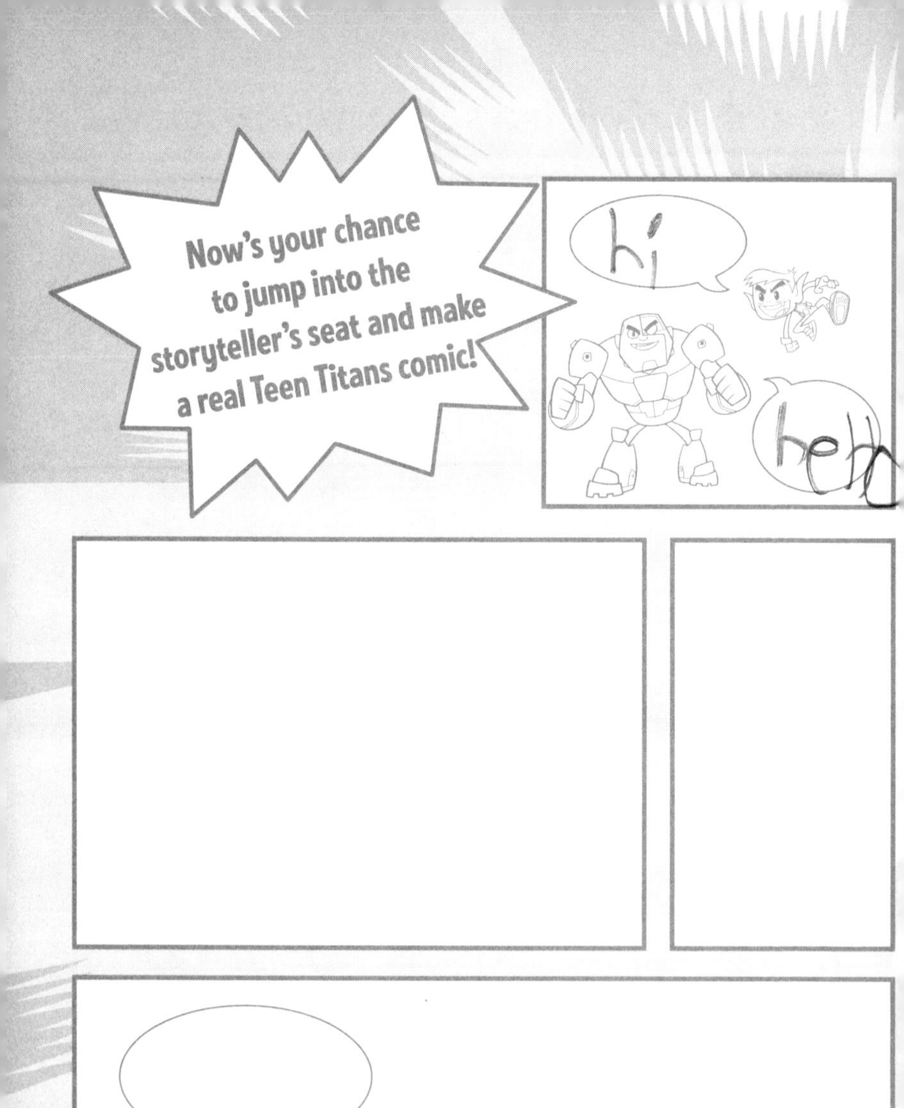
hi

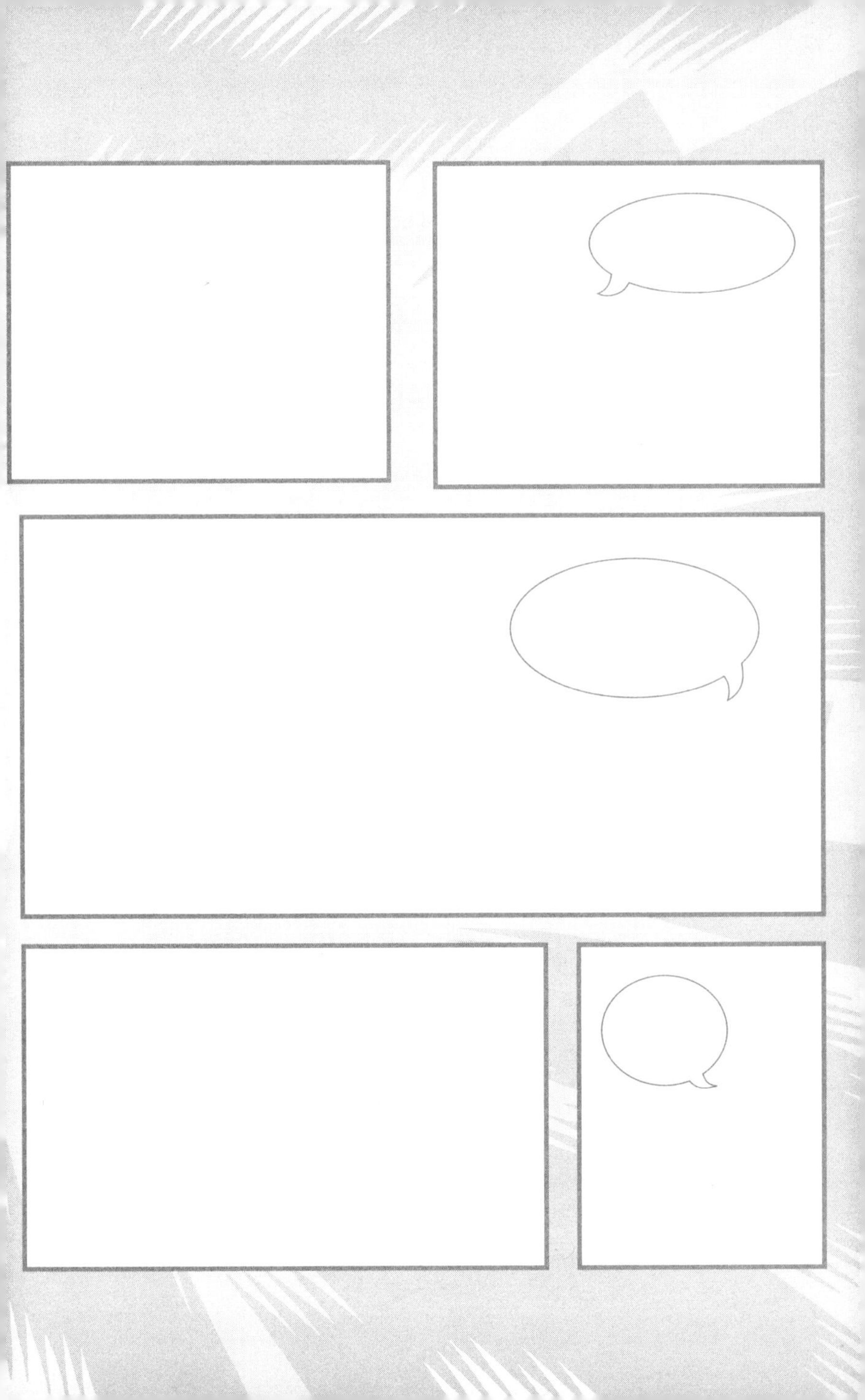

It's Cyborg's birthday, and the Teen Titans
are so excited!

Help them decorate the Tower and give him some presents.

At school, a substitute teacher causes the Teen Titans some real trouble. Draw a teacher who is sure to ruin their day!

Finish this drawing of Cyborg!

Raven is casting a spell, but something goes terribly wrong. All the Titans swap heads!

Color each mixed-up Teen Titan!

Jinx visits the Teen Titans, but she's really bad luck!

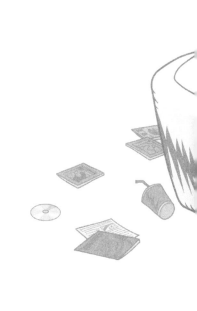

What does the Tower look like after Jinx has rolled through?

Draw your family and friends as a super hero team!

Cyborg builds a giant robot for the Titans to ride inside. What does it look like?

Aqualad takes the Teen Titans on a guided tour of the deep blue ocean.

Draw the sea life and other wonders they encounter!

Trigon visits Raven for her birthday and gives her a big present.

What does he give her?

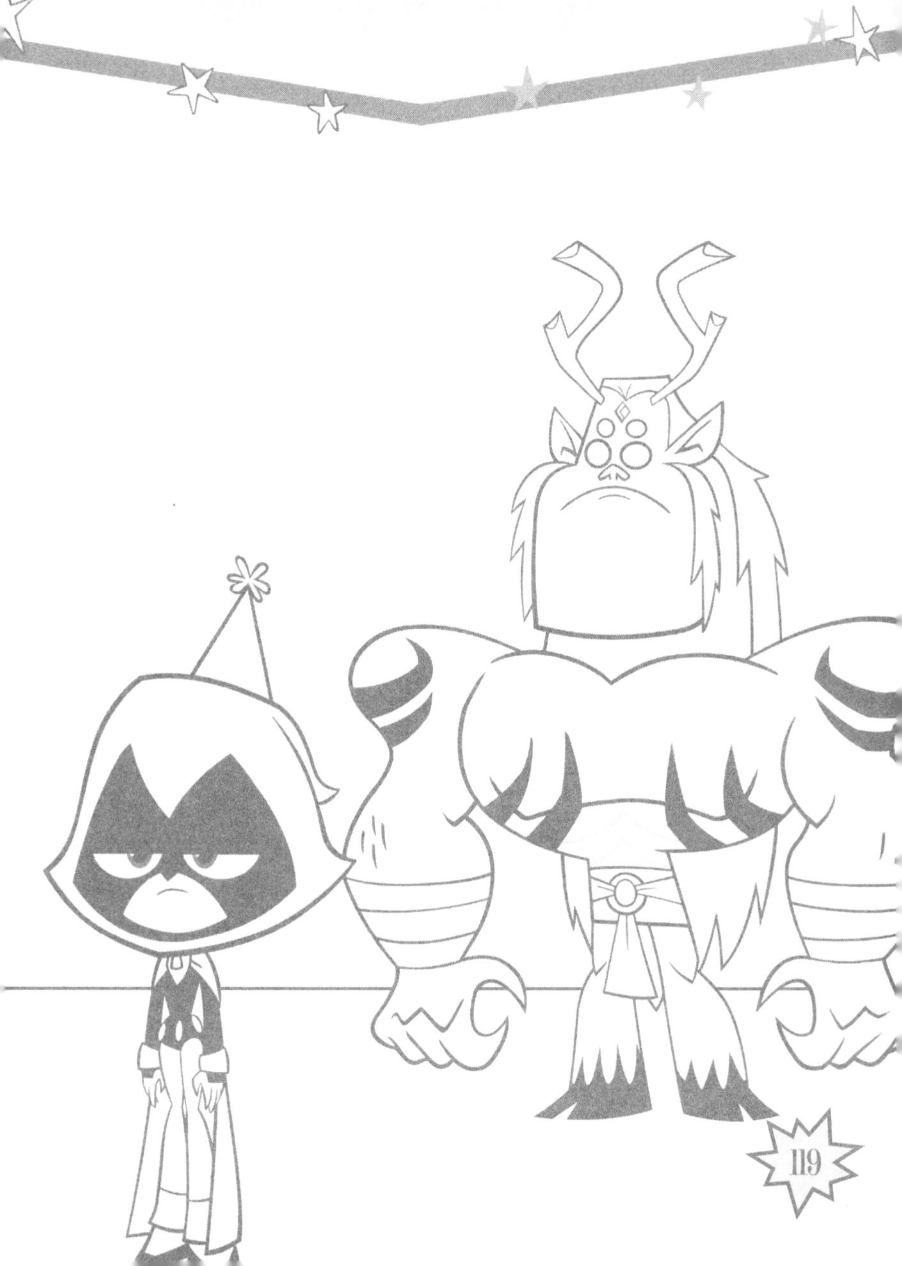

**Starfire, Cyborg, and Beast Boy are
all suffering from cape envy.**

Draw cool capes on them so they can be just like their cape-wearing cohorts.

Mumbo lures the Teen Titans to an old theater, where he puts on a special magic show just for them.

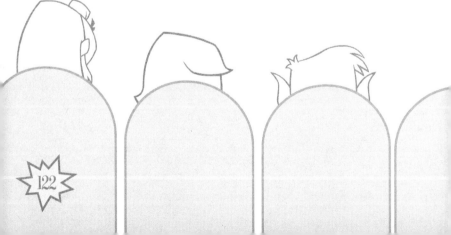

**Draw the curtains, lights, and rest of the stage
so Mumbo can put on a proper show.**

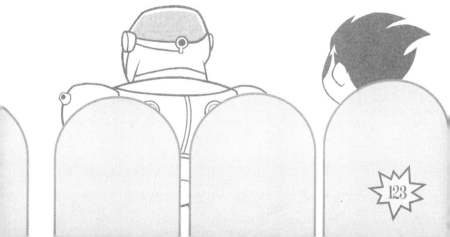

With a wave of his wand, Mumbo transforms the Teen Titans into cute little animals.

Draw the Titans in their furry, scaly, or feathery forms!

Mumbo lost his wand in a maze! If the Titans find the wand, they can break it and undo all his magic.

START

FINISH!

Help the Titans find the wand before Mumbo gets to it!

START

After a long day of fighting crime, the Teen Titans celebrate by treating themselves to pizza, pie, and ice cream! Draw their treats!